50p

123

This book
belongs to

....

....

The Pirate's Hat
and other stories

Written by Nicola Baxter, Alison Boyle and Nick Ellsworth

Illustrated by Bill Bolton, Daniel Howarth, Anna Leplar, Gill Roberts and Rory Tyger

Language consultant: Betty Root

Produced for Chad Valley Toys
242–246 Marylebone Road,
London, NW1 6JL

www.woolworths.co.uk

ISBN 978-1-4054-6687-5
Printed in China

Contents

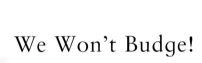

The Pirate's Hat

Each summer, Patrick used to go and stay with his Uncle Max and Auntie Jess, who lived in a tiny cottage by the sea.

One rainy afternoon, Patrick was indoors feeling a bit bored. Looking through Uncle Max's bookcase, he found a huge old book about pirates. Patrick settled into a comfy armchair, and began to read about one of the most dangerous pirates of all times, One-Armed Jake.

"I'm glad I'll never meet him," thought Patrick when he went to bed that night. "He's really scary!"

The next day was warm and sunny, and Patrick couldn't wait to go outdoors. He waved to Uncle Max and Auntie Jess, who were in the garden.

Then Patrick made his way down the steep, windy path to the beach.

After walking a little way along the sand, Patrick spotted a small gap in the cliff. He'd never noticed the gap before. It was the entrance to a small cave.

"It's very dark and cold in here," thought Patrick, as he stepped inside the cave. He shivered. "This feels a bit creepy."

Turning to leave, Patrick saw something half buried in the sand. He picked it up, and was amazed to see that it was an old and battered pirate's hat.

"Wow, a real pirate's hat!" cried Patrick,

putting it on his head.

Suddenly, he began to feel very tired. He lay down on the sandy floor of the cave and fell asleep straightaway.

When he woke up, Patrick quickly realized that he was no longer in the cave. He was lying on the deck of a ship – in the middle of a huge battle! The roar of the cannon was deafening and, all around him, men were yelling and fighting with swords. They were pirates! Patrick felt scared, and quickly hid behind a wooden barrel.

All of a sudden, a hand pulled Patrick out of his hiding-place. He found himself staring into the eyes of a pirate with only one arm.

"It's One-Armed Jake!" thought Patrick with horror.

"Come with me, lad. We've got work to do!" shouted One-Armed Jake fiercely, and he pushed Patrick roughly to the side of the ship.

Bobbing around in a small rowing boat in the sea below were two more pirates. Between them was a large wooden chest.

"Get in the rowing boat, lad. No funny tricks, mind! I'll be right behind you," snarled One-Armed Jake.

He pushed Patrick down a rope ladder and into the waiting boat. One-Armed Jake followed swiftly behind.

"Row, me shipmates, row!" yelled One-Armed Jake.

"Where are we going?" asked Patrick.

"To the beach to bury my money. See this chest, lad. My old enemy, Cap'n Saltwater, wants to steal it from me. That's what all the fighting's about!"

One-Armed Jake opened the box, and Patrick couldn't believe what he saw. Hundreds of gold coins lay glinting inside. From the corner of his eye, Patrick noticed a single gold coin in the bottom of the boat. He quickly picked it up and put it in his pocket, hoping that none of the pirates had been watching.

When they arrived at the beach, Patrick and the pirates dragged the heavy chest towards a nearby cave.

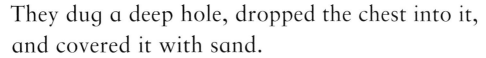

They dug a deep hole, dropped the chest into it, and covered it with sand.

"Cap'n Saltwater will never get his hands on my treasure now!" laughed One-Armed Jake.

"What about the boy? He knows exactly where the treasure's hidden!" growled one pirate, who had a huge scar across one cheek. "He could tell anybody where it is, or even come back and steal it for himself."

"That's true," yelled One-Armed Jake, looking at Patrick with his cold eyes. "Maybe we should bury him with the treasure."

Now Patrick felt really frightened.

"But, before we do anything," continued One-Armed Jake, "the boy's got something of mine!"

"Oh, no!" thought Patrick. "He knows about the coin in my pocket." Patrick trembled. "I'm in for it now."

"The boy's got my favourite . . . HAT!" roared One-Armed Jake, and grabbed it off Patrick's head.

At that moment, there was a huge flash, and Patrick closed his eyes.

When he opened them again, the pirates were nowhere to be seen. Patrick was lying alone in the cave, with One-Armed Jake's hat by his side. Everything seemed to be back to normal again.

Patrick sat up and rubbed his eyes.

"What a scary dream!" he thought. "And yet it seemed so real."

Patrick picked up the hat and ran back up to the cottage to tell Uncle Max and Auntie Jess what had happened.

"How terrifying! I'm glad it was just a dream," said Uncle Max, after listening to Patrick's story during tea.

All of a sudden, something fell out of Patrick's pocket. When the three of them saw what it was, they all gasped with surprise.

There on the floor, glinting in the sunlight, lay a shiny, bright gold coin.

16

A Drink for
Draggle Dragon

On a hot, hot day, the only thing a grown-up dragon wants to do is crawl into her cool, dark cave and have a long snooooooozzze. Lovely!

But little dragons are just like you and me. They don't want to sleep on a beautiful afternoon. They want to whizzzzzz around the mountain paths, and zoooooom over the rocks and sliiiiiide down the slopes.

One day, after whizzing and zooming and sliding under the sizzling hot sun, Draggle Dragon flopped down on the mountainside. What he needed more than anything else was a long, cool drink.

Down in the valley, sparkling in the sunshine, was a deep mountain lake. Under the surface, the water was dark and cold. A drink of it would be delicious.

Draggle sighed. He remembered what his mother had told him, over and over again.

"Never," she always said, looking serious and stern, "drink anything but juniper juice. And drink it through a straw. That is the only safe drink for dragons."

It was a long way back to the cave and the juniper juice.

Draggle crept down a winding path, closer and closer to the cold, blue water. As he watched, some little birds skimmed over the water's surface, dipping

their beaks to take a drink. Surely, if little birds could drink the water, it would be safe for a dragon?

Draggle went right up to the edge of the lake. He dipped one toe in the water. Ooooh! It was lovely! And nothing bad happened to his toe at all.

"Excuse me!" said a polite little voice. And a small deer trotted around the side of Draggle and began to drink from the lake.

Tiny birds could drink the water. Delicate deer could drink the water. Draggle made up his mind. He couldn't think of a single reason why he shouldn't drink it too.

The naughty little dragon cupped his paws and scooped some water towards his mouth. Most of it dripped out between his claws, but a few precious, sparkling drops went in. It was sooooo good.

19

Nothing horrible happened. But it would take ages to drink a lot this way. Draggle decided to risk it. He leaned forward and dipped his face in the lake. And as the clear, cold water rushed into his mouth, something horrible did happen.

Pffffft!

Draggle's flames went out! All dragons breathe fire. They are so used to it that they don't even think about it. But they are careful when they walk through the forest, and dragons don't have curtains in their caves!

Pfffft!

Draggle breathed hard. He thought his flames might come back. But they didn't. He tried coughing and sneezing and shaking his head. But it didn't work.

As he ran home, he began to panic. What would his mother say?

She said a lot. Some of the politer words she used were "Dunklebrain", "Google" and "Durkdragon".

Draggle waited until she paused. "Is there anything we can do?" he asked in a tiny voice.

Draggle's mother sighed. "It's dangerous. It's unpleasant. And it serves you right," she said. "We have to go to the volcano."

The journey to the volcano was long and tiring. And a journey always feels longer when your mother is muttering about you the whole way. But there are worse things than muttering. A roaring mountain spitting out stones and red-hot fire is worse, for a start.

Draggle was very frightened of the volcano.

"Stop whimpering, Draggle," said his mother.

"This is what we must do. We fly over the top – quickly, of course – and, as we pass over the big hole in the middle, you must take a big breath in. That will light up your flames again."

Draggle had never been so scared in his life. He wondered if perhaps he could live without flames after all. No! A dragon must breathe fire or he is nothing better than a big, lumpy lizard. Draggle gulped and took off.

Flapping over the volcano, keeping close behind his mother, Draggle didn't dare to look down. "Breathe in now!" shouted his mother. Draggle breathed in – and felt as if his whole body was on fire.

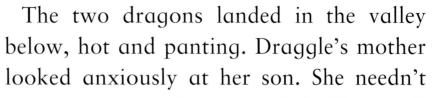

The two dragons landed in the valley below, hot and panting. Draggle's mother looked anxiously at her son. She needn't have worried. The small dragon was himself again. Little flickers of orange fire came out of his nose in a perfectly normal way.

"I hope you've learned your lesson, Draggle," said his mother. "Now, let's go home and have some juniper juice."

"Yes, Mum," replied Draggle. But as they trotted along the valley, one very silly little dragon kept looking at the sparkling water of a little stream rushing along beside them. Luckily, bigger dragons sometimes have very special powers.

"Don't even think about it, Draggle," said his mother.

23

We Won't Budge!

It was a hot, hot day in a hot, hot country. The watering-holes were definitely the coolest place to be. But there had been no rain for days, so there was just enough water for one group of animals at a time to stand in the watering-hole. The animals decided to take turns. Today it was the turn of the hippos, and one thing was for sure . . . the hippos were definitely not going to budge.

"We're cool," they gloated noisily to the other animals.

"Pleeeease!" whined the sweating vultures near the edge of the water. "Pleeeease could we have an incy-wincy turn?"

But the hippos just chanted: "We won't budge!" So the vultures tap-tap-tapped on the hippos' hard skin with their sharp beaks to teach them a lesson. But hippos are thick skinned in more ways than one, and they didn't feel a thing.

"Pleasssssssse!" hissed the snakes, slithering near the edge of the water. "Pleasssssssse could we have a slithery slice of a turn?"

But the hippos just chanted: "We won't budge!"

"We won't budge!"

So the snakes coiled their long bodies tightly round the hippos' legs and tried to pull them out!

25

But hippos are strong in more ways than one, and they won't ever move unless they want to.

"Plehee-hee-ease!" neighed the zebras, hoping for a tiny share of the water. "Plehee-hee-ease could we have the thinnest stripe of a turn?"

But the hippos just chanted: "We won't budge!"
So the zebras all pawed at the ground with their hooves, trying to scare the hippos away. But hippos are brave in more ways than one, and they didn't even blink an eyelid. And one thing was for sure . . . and they said it again, "WE WON'T BUDGE!"

"WE WON'T BUDGE!"

As the sun grew hotter, more and more animals came to the watering-hole. They stood around its edge, staring across at the selfish hippos. But the hippos weren't going to budge even for the gentle antelopes, who helped them out by swatting flies from their ears with their swishing tails. Today, those cool hippos standing in the cool water of the watering-hole were not going to budge – for anyone!

Suddenly there came a noise that made the hippos look up. Every ear of every hippo twitched, and listened. It was a noise that made the antelopes and zebras and snakes and vultures sprint and gallop and slither and fly away in an instant.

DER-UM! DER-UM! DR-UM! DR-UM!

DRM! DRM! DRM!

The hippos stood up. Their eyes grew wider, and their great strong legs trembled. Their hard skins shivered, and they didn't know what to do.

DER-UM!   DER-UM!   DER-UM!   DER-UM!

"Help!" whispered the littlest hippo very quietly.

"We won't budge," whispered the biggest hippo even more quietly.

There was silence, except for the thundering dust-cloud approaching the watering-hole.

"WE WILL BUDGE!" exclaimed all the hippos together, as they rushed away.

The thundering dust was in fact an enormous herd of heavy elephants. They were thirsty and hot, and they weren't going to be put off cooling their feet. So the elephants carried on running towards the watering-hole until they splashed right into the middle of the pool.

"Aaaaah!" sighed the elephants, trumpeting their happiness. And all the other animals (except those brave old hippos) sneaked back to take a look at them.

"One thing is definitely for sure," called the sweating vultures. "Those cool elephants are not going to budge for anyone."

But it didn't matter, because the elephants saw how hot and bothered the vultures and the snakes and the antelopes were under the scorching sun. They counted: "One and . . . two and . . . three and . . .". Then they sucked up the water into their long bendy trunks, pointed, squinted, aimed and fired the water at the animals all around.

"Aaaah!" "Aaaah!" sighed the antelopes.
"Aaaah!" neighed the zebras.
"Aaaah!" hissed the snakes.
"Aaaah!" croaked the vultures.

29

"Aaaaaaah!" sighed the hippos, who were standing a long way off, watching everything. If only they could be sprayed too. And slowly, very slowly, hardly knowing what they were doing, the hot hippos made their way back to the watering-hole.

But there was only room for one group of animals at a time to stand in the water. Now it was the elephants' turn. And one thing was for sure . . . "WE WON'T BUDGE!" they called out, when they saw the hippos approaching.

"Pleeeeeeeeease!" pleaded the hippos. "Plehee-hee-ease could we have the chunkiest chunk of a turn?"

"No you can't!" trumped the cool elephants. "That's just greedy."

"Hurrah!" cheered the antelopes, the snakes, the zebras and the vultures. They all remembered very well that the hippos didn't budge for them – or squirt them.

30

So the hot hippos, with their burning hot skins, tramped away from the watering-hole. And the elephants watched them go, and felt very sorry for them. They counted: "One and . . . two and . . . three and . . .". Then they sucked up the water into their long bendy trunks, pointed, squinted, aimed and fired at the hippos.

"ONE! TWO! THREE!"

"Aaaaaaaaaaaaaaaaaah!" sighed the hippos.

And one thing was for sure . . . they were definitely NOT going to budge.

"Aaaaaaaah!"

Ug-Ug-Ugly

Long, long, long ago, a huge egg lay in a nest. The egg wobbled, then wobbled a bit more. It rolled a bit, then rolled a bit more. It rolled right over the edge of the nest – WOOOOOOOOO!

Bump!

Plick!

C r a c k!

Out popped a wrinkly, bobble-eyed, ugly-faced baby dinosaur. He squinted at the wide world all around. Everything looked scary. Through the leaves peeped

one,

two,

three,

four

wrinkly, bobble-eyed, ugly-faced toddler dinosaurs. They stared at the new baby as he began to wriggle out of his eggshell.

"Ug!" said the first toddler.

"Ug!" said the second.

"Ug!" said the third.

"Ug!" said the fourth, nodding her head. "You're UGLY!"

The baby dinosaur stood up on his thin new legs, and crept away into the shadow of a dark drooping flower.

The toddler dinosaurs skipped off happily, calling:

"Bye for now!"

"Little monster!"

"Come and find us!"

"See you soon!"

Then through the trees burst a wrinkly, bobble-eyed, ugly-faced mummy dinosaur.

"La-di-da!" sang Mummy, "my egg should be hatched by now – la-di-da!"

But when she peered into her nest,

"Uh?" said Mummy. "Where's my baby?"

And **thump! thump! thump!** she trudged off through the steamy forest to look for him. She thumped round the bursting volcano, across the gushing river and through the gurgling swamp, but

she couldn't find her baby anywhere.

So Mummy sat down and frowned, and forced her pea-sized brain to think. And think it did. It thought about an egg. It thought about an eggshell.

"EGGSHELL!" she exclaimed, as she thump, thump, thumped back through the gurgling swamp, across the gushing river, round the bursting volcano and through the steamy forest to the place where she had built her nest.

This time she didn't look inside the nest, but on the ground below it.

"Eggshell!" she whispered, when she spotted a fleck of shiny green shell.

"Eggshell!" she announced, when she spotted more flecks of shell farther along.

"Uh?" said Mummy when the trail of eggshell stopped.

She sat down and frowned, and forced her pea-sized brain to think. And think it did. It thought about a baby.

"WHERE'S MY BABY?" called Mummy at the top of her voice.

"Here we are!" replied her four wrinkly, bobble-eyed, ugly-faced toddler dinosaurs.

"You're not babies!" she said. "I'm talking about the baby who came out of that eggshell. He must be here somewhere."

The toddlers all

silently pointed towards the same place.

Mummy dinosaur gently lifted the head of a dark drooping flower and, curled up in a ball, was her baby.

"Ug!" said the first toddler.

"Ug!" began the second, before Mummy interrupted.

"My baby!" Mummy cried, as she gathered the dinosaur in her huge claws. She looked round proudly at all her ugly children. "Isn't he lovely?" admired Mummy. "What shall we call him?"

"Ugly?" suggested one of the toddlers.

"Don't be so unkind!" scolded Mummy, stroking her newly hatched baby. "Poor little thing – fancy thinking of that!"

"Eggshell?" suggested another, as the baby gurgled loudly.

"He likes that name!" all the toddler dinosaurs called out together.

Mummy sat down and frowned, and forced her pea-sized brain to think. And think it did.

It thought about a perfect name for her baby dinosaur. It thought of the long journey Mummy had made to find him.

And the name she came up with was . . .

"GURGLING SWAMP!"

She called out the name at the top of her voice, as the baby gave a huge burp.

"Yay!" cheered the toddlers, who thought it was a very good name for the wrinkly, bobble-eyed, ugly-faced baby dinosaur who was happily burping (or gurgling) in his mummy's arms.

Pansy Pig

One squiggly, wriggly piglet can get into lots of trouble. Two squiggly, wriggly piglets are worse! Can you imagine what six squiggly, wriggly piglets might do? Poor Mrs Pig didn't have to imagine. From the moment her six piglets were born, they were trouble!

There was Percy, who just loved to stick his little pink snout into lots of things he should not.

There was Penny, who liked to explore . . . everything!

There was little Pickle, who was always getting lost.

There were Poppy and Pippa, the terrible two, who tried to eat the strangest things.

And there was Pansy, who got into more trouble than the other five piglets put together.

Now Pansy wasn't naughtier than Percy. She wasn't sillier than Poppy or Pippa. She certainly wasn't as brave as Penny and Pickle. So why did Mrs Pig have to give Pansy a "serious talk" at least three times a day?

Well, the other little pigs were as alike as five peas in a pod. They were squiggly and wriggly and wiggly and pink. They were pink all over from their twisty tails to their sniffly snouts. It was very, very hard to tell the five piglets apart.

Pansy was different. She was pink, too, but on her little pink bottom she had a brown splodge. It looked just like a pansy flower!

When Mrs Pig saw four little pink bottoms sticking out of the horse trough, munching something they shouldn't, she couldn't be sure who three of them were. But one little bottom had a beautiful brown pansy on it.

"PANSY!" yelled Mrs Pig. "Come out of that trough right now! And you too . . . er . . . you other three!"

It was the same when Mrs Pig saw five little piglets diving in the duck pond, upsetting the dabbling ducks. Four of the piglets looked just the same. But one little piglet, who was splashily practising the piggy paddle, had a very familiar flower on her bottom.

"PANSY!" screeched Mrs Pig. "Come out of that pond right now! And you too . . . er . . . you other four!"

The ducks, the horses and the hens got used to hearing Mrs Pig shouting at all hours of the day and night.

"Pansy! PANSY! P-A-N-S-Y!"

The other squiggly piglets got used to it too. But Pansy didn't. It wasn't fair that she always got the blame . . . just because she was different.

Then, one drippy, droppy, drizzly day, all six piglets got tired of staying in their pigsty and looking out at the rain.

"I'm going to explore!" squeaked Penny. She trotted out into the rain.

"Wait for me!" cried Pickle, scrambling after her.

"Can you eat rain?" squealed Poppy and Pippa, and scampered off to see.

"Let's splash in the puddles!" squeaked Percy, dashing out of doors.

And Pansy Pig, who didn't want to be left behind, rushed after him.

For the rest of the morning, six wet and wiggly piglets had a wonderful time. When they found that the bank of the pond was one big muddy playground, they couldn't believe their luck.

"Whee!" they skidded and slipped.

"Whoo!" they splished and sploshed.

"Whaa!" they rolled and wriggled.

When Mrs Pig came looking for six naughty little pink pigs, she couldn't find them at all. But she did see six dirty brown piglets covered in mud.

43

Mrs Pig opened her mouth to yell . . . and then shut it again. She couldn't be sure. Were these really her piglets? She looked for Pansy's familiar little bottom, but all she saw was mud, mud and more mud.

Mrs Pig tried to feel cross. But even when a big splodge of mud came flying across and hit her on the

ear, she couldn't manage it. She started to laugh. And the next minute, she couldn't resist it any longer. She jumped with a splat right into the mud and squiggled and wriggled herself.

"I love getting muddy!" squealed Pansy Pig.

"So do I!" laughed Mrs Pig.

And a squiggly wriggly little piglet, who hadn't been shouted at all day, gave her big muddy mum a big muddy hug.